Hold You

To:

From:

Text copyright © 2021 by Craig Lucie

Published by: InTandem Digital Press
intandemdigitalpress.com

Illustrations and Cover by Nai Saechao
Contact Nai at naiyhansae@gmail.com

ISBN: 978-1-7377374-1-4

Library of Congress: 9781737737407

Publisher's Cataloging-in-Publication data

Names: Lucie, Craig, author. | Saechao, Nai, illustrator.
Title: Hold you / by Craig Lucie ; illustrated by Nai Saechao.
Description: Atlanta, GA: InTandem Digital Press, 2021. |
Summary: Have your kids said, "hold you!" when they really
mean, "hold me?" Hold You is one father's nostalgic storytelling of
his daughter's endearing phrase that was just too cute to correct.
It is a reminder to us all to make time for each other.
Identifiers: LCCN: 2021917702 | ISBN: 978-1-7377374-1-4 (hardcover) |
978-1-7377374-0-7 (paperback) | 978-1-7377374-2-1 (ebook)
Subjects: LCSH Father and child--Juvenile fiction. | Family--Juvenile fiction. | CYAC
Father and child--Fiction. | Family--Fiction. | BISAC JUVENILE FICTION / Family /
General | JUVENILE FICTION / Social Themes / General | JUVENILE FICTION /
Family / Parents
Classification: LCC PZ7.1.L832 Ho 2021 | DDC [E]--dc23

Hold You

WRITTEN BY CRAIG LUCIE   ILLUSTRATED BY NAI SAECHAO

**InTandem
Digital
Press**

To Alexandra, Adrienne & Liam —
my 'why' behind everything I do.

To my parents who held me when I said,
"Hold You Me!"
And to YOU, the reader, to always remember
to pause and hold those you love most...
both young and old.

- C.L.

To my forever puppy, Snowwhite - N.S.

I remember when you were born
and the moment I first held you.

I remember our first night together
and the look in your eyes,

Admiring you while reading and
singing sweet, sweet lullabies.

I remember when we left the hospital and your first trip in the car;

Being a little nervous, but knowing home wasn't too far.

I remember you meeting new family and friends and seeing how much you were already loved.

I knew from the beginning you were a true gift from above.

Your first steps seem like yesterday as you reached for us, arms held wide.

We were always there to catch you, knowing one day you'd leave our side.

Your first words were as simple as can be, but were oh, so special to your mommy and me.

And when you needed a hug or hold, it was those two words that got me most.

Hold you!
Hold you!
Hold you!

I thought many times about correcting you to say "hold me" instead,

But each time I stopped, because it sounded so sweet in my head.

Everywhere we went, you waddled with glee to explore.

But when I heard those two words, I knew you needed more.

Hold you!
Hold you!
Hold you!

I remember reaching down for you, so I could hold you tight.

I knew time was flying by me, like the wind behind a kite.

These two very special words will always bring a smile to my face,

And bring back all the joy of a far off, happy place.

Hold you!
Hold you!
Hold you!

And one day when you're older and the past so far away,

You will be stronger and wiser...And I'll be the one to say.

Hold me!
Hold me!
Hold me!

CRAIG LUCIE lives in Atlanta, Georgia with his wife and two children. Craig has over 20 years of experience as a broadcast journalist and reporter. He has won an EMMY for Best News Anchor and has been named Best On-Air Personality in the southeast. After almost two decades in the news business, Craig Lucie started his company, 'Lucie,' which means light and illumination. He and his team use their news and communications background to create compelling content to shine light on all the good that businesses, nonprofits, and individuals are doing every day. To learn more, visit LucieContent.com.

NAI SAECHAO is a children's book illustrator based in Northern California. When she's not sketching, revising, or painting, she loves to spend time in cafes with good company and a strong cup of coffee. Contact Nai at naiyhansae@gmail.com

CPSIA information can be obtained
at www.ICGtesting.com
Printed in the USA
BVHW051121021121
620551BV00007B/964